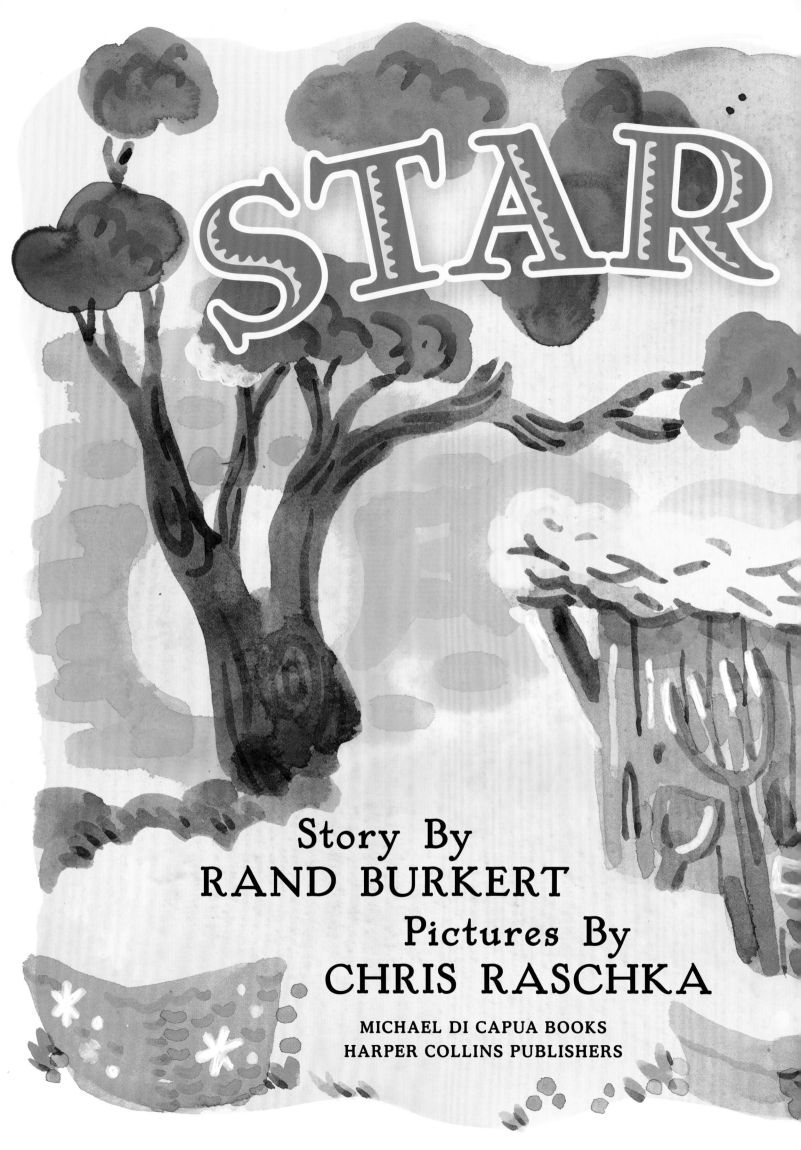

STAR

Story By
RAND BURKERT
Pictures By
CHRIS RASCHKA

MICHAEL DI CAPUA BOOKS
HARPER COLLINS PUBLISHERS

For Mom
R.B.

For Lydie
C.R.

Text © 2023 by Rand Burkert • Pictures © 2023 by Chris Raschka • Library of Congress control number: 2022941729
HarperCollins Publishers, New York, NY 10007 • Printed and bound in Italy by Rotolito • Designed by Steve Scott
First edition, 2023 • 23 24 25 26 27 RTLO 6 5 4 3 2 1

At evening, patterns made of stars appear
to curious eyes. Constellations,
as we call them, seem to us
mysterious. They answer, though,
to names that you can know.
Taurus, the Bull. Cancer, the Crab.
And the Hunter. Who is he? His name
is also in this book. So turn the page.
Two rustic guides are kind enough
to take you up to far-off Space.
A donkey and his farmer know the way
to starry darkness, from Earth's sunlit day.

Meet Giovanni and Lorenzo,
Specialists in Sky Repair.
Here they are, walking on air
over the Moon
and out past Mars,
searching for holes to fill with stars.

"Steady, don't spill," Giovanni says.
Lorenzo brays. He stumbles.
"Steady, friend!" The baskets sway.
Star stuff hisses, sparks and sprays.

"Now, *there's* an empty spot!
What do you say, old friend?"
Lorenzo brays, he kicks.
Giovanni pitches star stuff
out into the dark—
and there it stays,
it sticks!

The star stuff grows!
Hot, round, bright,
it warms Lorenzo's nose.
"A star, old friend," Giovanni says.
"We've done it again."

But then, a scare!
"Lorenzo, you've put your foot
in something awful there!
A nebula!" Giovanni cries.
"A nebula has got your leg! Pull it out!"
Poor Lorenzo tries.
He kicks, he brays.
"Count on me," Giovanni says.
"I'll get you free."

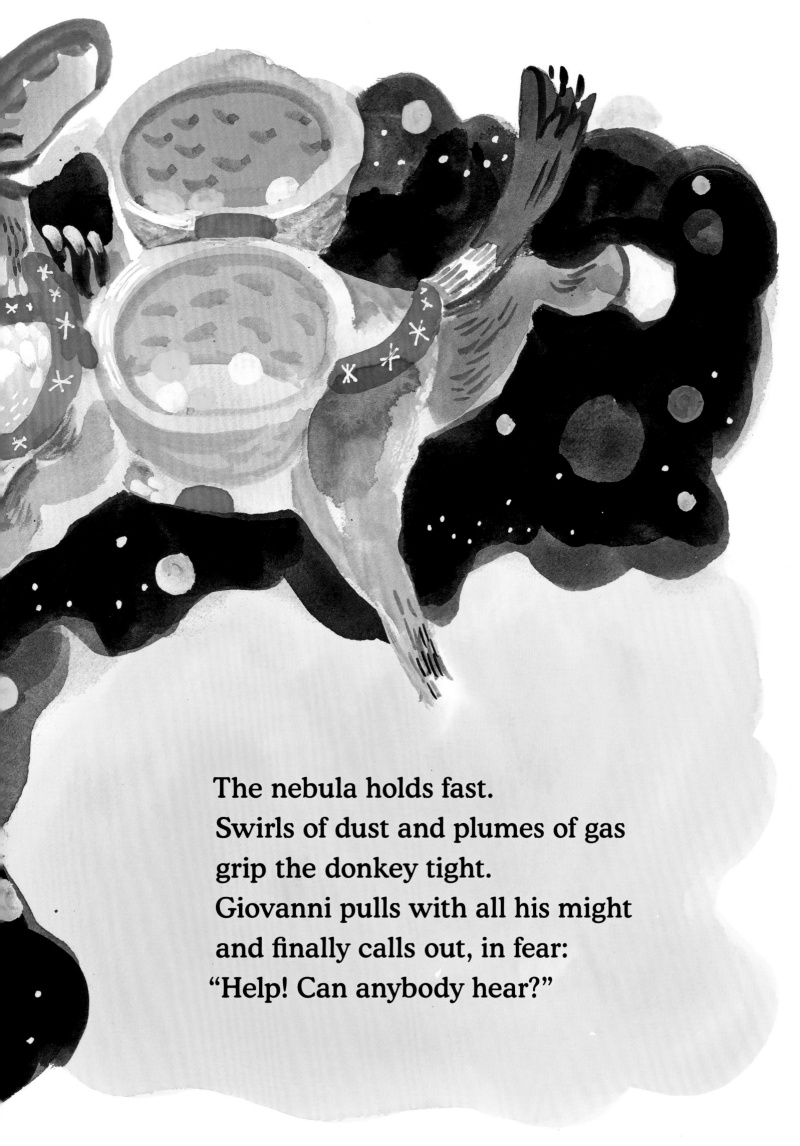

The nebula holds fast.
Swirls of dust and plumes of gas
grip the donkey tight.
Giovanni pulls with all his might
and finally calls out, in fear:
"Help! Can anybody hear?"

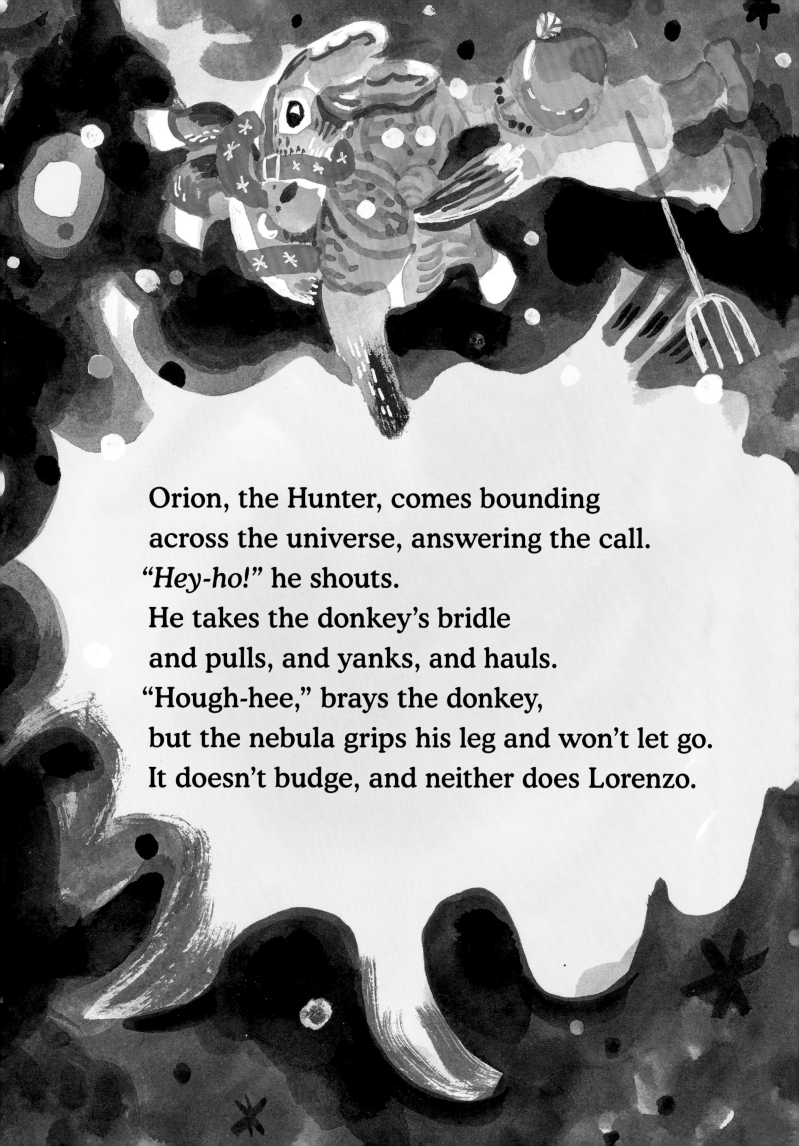

Orion, the Hunter, comes bounding
across the universe, answering the call.
"Hey-ho!" he shouts.
He takes the donkey's bridle
and pulls, and yanks, and hauls.
"Hough-hee," brays the donkey,
but the nebula grips his leg and won't let go.
It doesn't budge, and neither does Lorenzo.

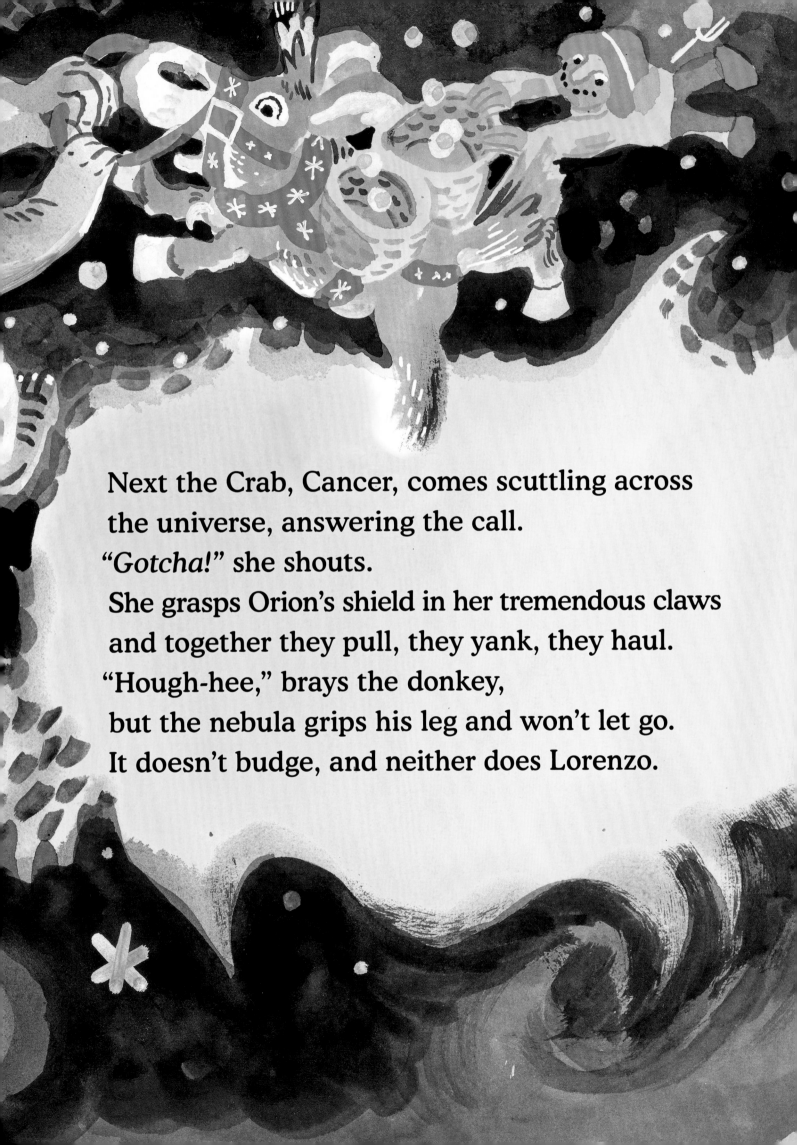

Next the Crab, Cancer, comes scuttling across
the universe, answering the call.
"Gotcha!" she shouts.
She grasps Orion's shield in her tremendous claws
and together they pull, they yank, they haul.
"Hough-hee," brays the donkey,
but the nebula grips his leg and won't let go.
It doesn't budge, and neither does Lorenzo.

Finally the Great Bull, Taurus,
comes charging across the universe,
answering the call.
"*Grab a horn!*" he shouts to the Crab.

He pulls, and she yanks Orion,
who hauls Lorenzo, who kicks and moans.
"Hee-hough," he groans.
And what do you know?

THE NEBULA
LETS GO!

Hurrah! Lorenzo is free!
He shakes his flanks.
Giovanni bows, he gives his thanks:
"I'll remember this to the end of my days."

"Speak nothing of it," Orion says.
"Piece of cake," says the Crab.
And last of all, says Taurus,
"You would have done the same for us."

Giovanni takes Lorenzo's bridle
and leads him down, down,
out of the starry night,
down over mountains,
down to Earth,
to see the good Sun rise.

"Here's a tree I love
and flowers for you to eat!
We deserve a rest,
and you deserve a treat.
There's our old Sun,
high above the sea,
best star ever made
—if you ask me."